JURASSIC WORLD

pi kids ®

An imprint of Phoenix International Publications, Inc.

Chicago • London • New York • Hamburg • Mexico City • Sydney

Jurassic World reminds humans just how small they really are. Although Apatosaurus towers over tourists—she's as tall as a two-story house and as long as two school buses— she prefers to graze peacefully.

While Apatosaurus feeds on hard-to-reach leaves, gaze about Isla Nublar and locate these other creatures in Gyrosphere Valley:

Stegosaurus pair | young Apatosaurus | this Triceratops | baby Triceratops | this Parasaurolophus | these tourists

Although Mosasaurus is not scientifically a dinosaur—technically, she is an early ancestor of monitor lizards like the Komodo dragon—the aquatic terror draws a crowd. She lurks beneath the surface, waiting to feed her voracious appetite and leave the guests in awe.

As Mosasaurus prepares to feast, find these astonished faces in the crowd:

The magic behind Jurassic World is actually...science! First, Park scientists refined the de-extinction process and brought dinosaurs back to life. Now, they are working on something new: the first-ever hybrid dinosaur. They combine the DNA of dinosaurs and modern animals to make an unforgettable attraction.

While the scientists work, look around the lab for these hatching Stygimoloch eggs:

The science behind Jurassic World is fascinating, but a trip through Gyrosphere Valley reveals different wonders...like a herd of Ankylosaurus. These impressive grazers weigh more than an African elephant and eat more than 130 pounds of ferns a day!

While the herd packs it in, pick out these particular Ankylosaurus:

Oh, no! Indominus rex has broken out of her enclosure! The first hybrid dinosaur is on the loose and causing trouble with the Ankylosaurus. The herbivores are covered in bony deposits called osteoderms, but will this armor be enough to protect them from Indominus?

While Indominus is distracted, locate these park authorities trying to contain the situation:

Things have gone from bad to worse! The flying dinosaurs have broken free from the Aviary, and they are soaring towards the tourists. Pteranodons do not have teeth, but their sharp beaks can do a lot of damage. The park is no longer safe for guests. Time to evacuate!

Spot these specific Pteranodons before they make it to the crowds:

With the humans gone, Isla Nublar belongs to the dinosaurs, and a new food chain begins to establish itself. Herbivores like the three-horned Triceratops must defend themselves and their young from carnivores like Carnotaurus. And carnivores like Carnotaurus must stay alert for even bigger rivals...like T. rex!

As the dinosaurs duke it out, keep an eye open for these other island inhabitants now wandering freely:

Baryonyx   **Pachycephalosaurus**   **Brachiosaurus**   **Blue**   **Stiggy**   **Dilophosaurus**

Dinosaurs rule their own world now that the people have fled. With high intelligence, Velociraptors like Blue are particularly suited to survive without humans. Although Jurassic World began in a lab, nature has taken hold. Life...finds a way.

As Blue surveys her surroundings, search the ruins for these remnants of a bygone era:

tattered tee   **shattered gyrosphere**   **discarded ATV**   **abandoned bike**   **permanently off-road vehicle**   **lost toy**

Apatosaurus likes to feast on ferns. Head back to the herd and find these leafy snacks:

monstera   cycadeoidea   anthurium   conifer   cycad   tree fern

Mosasaurus is amazing! Guests want to remember this and other Jurassic World wonders forever, so they visit the gift shop for souvenirs. Return to the Lagoon and locate these keepsakes:

Jurassic World t-shirt   stuffed Stegosaurus   balloon Brontosaurus   T. rex action figure   Dilophosaurus squirt gun   Triceratops high-tops

Scientific breakthroughs come from lots of research. Go back to the lab and investigate this important work:

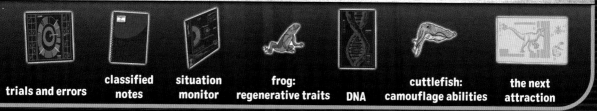

trials and errors   classified notes   situation monitor   frog: regenerative traits   DNA   cuttlefish: camouflage abilities   the next attraction

Dinosaurs tend to leave their mark on the world. Head back to Gyrosphere Valley and pick out these sets of footprints:

Indominus rex cuts a terrifying figure. Head back to the battle and find these fleeing dinosaurs:

Pteranodons do not have teeth, but Dimorphodons do. Hurry back to the Aviary and locate these fanged fliers:

Without labs to hatch their eggs, the dinosaurs have begun nesting. Creep back to the dinosaur battle and locate these nests:

Nature fills all niches. Venture back to the Visitor Center and find these Compsognathus that have moved in:

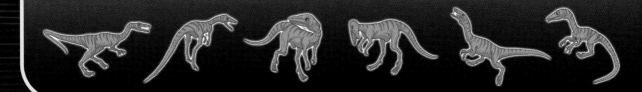